LIVING ON A MILITARY BASE

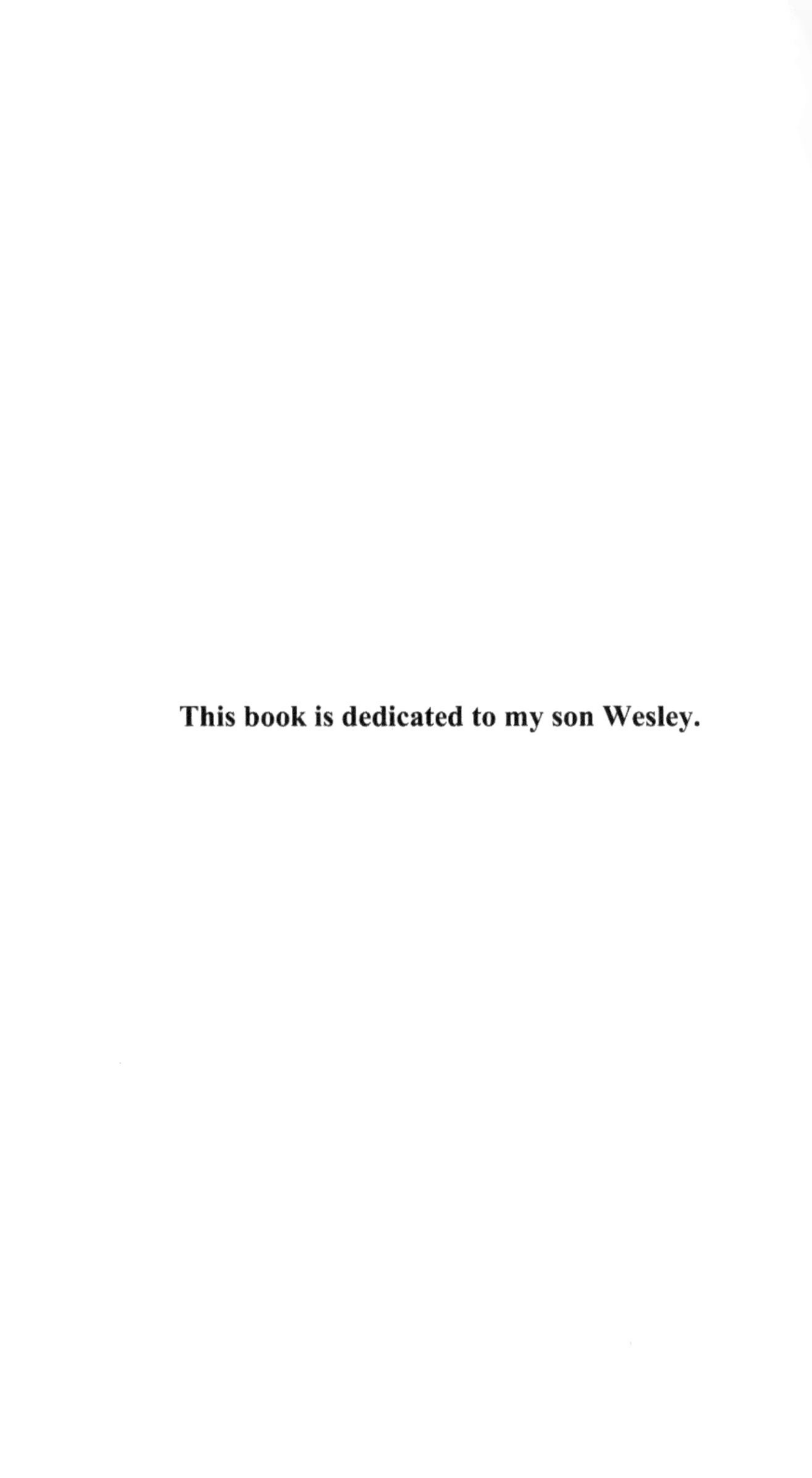

This book is dedicated to my son Wesley.

Table Of Contents

My Life

My name is **Wesley.** I am eleven years old. I have two brothers. My brothers are fifteen and twelve years old. We live on an island near Japan called Okinawa. Okinawa is an island which is about sixty-seven miles long and seventeen miles wide. I go to school off base at Maranatha Baptist Church Academy. We live on an Air Force Base called "Kadena Air Force Base." I was born in a Navy base hospital called "Camp Lester" which is in Chatan-Cho. My dad's Aunt (Leslie) was born in the same hospital. I found out that my dad's grandfather (John) lived on Kadena Air Force Base too, in the past. He was in the Air Force. This is my dad's second tour to Kadena Air Base. My mom works in the kitchen part time at the Tee House which is near the golf course.

This Is The Naval Hospital At Camp Lester Where I Was Born

Tee House On Kadena Air Force Base Where My Mom Worked Part Time

Aerial Map of Okinawa

This map shows where I live on Okinawa. Okinawa is in the sea all by itself at the bottom of Japan surrounded by water, which of course makes typhoons ripe for coming to the island.

My Dad's Military Job

My dad is in the Air Force. His prior job was as a Law Enforcement Specialist in the Air Force, but now he has a different job called Logistics Specialist. He loads aircraft, makes sure people are ready to go on temporary duty, and trains other people to prepare for wartime and peacetime activities. Sometimes, my dad must plan and play war games. He must go away sometimes for temporary duty assignments in the Air Force. I miss him when he is gone, and it is difficult to be without him.

Our Friends

We have friends named the "Belton's." Their mom is in the U.S. Marines. They have seven kids. Sometimes, we go out to dinner together at the Non-Commissioned Officers Club. We would have ten children and four adults at the table. I used to feel sorry for the server. Sometimes, we would go to Camp Futenma to visit them and play. There were so many kids to play with.

Life on a Military Base

Living on a military base like Kadena is so exceptional. It is like a big city that has a plethora of activities to take part in. There are exciting adventures to explore on and off base. Military members can sign up for tours of the island at the Base Tour Office. These tours are fun. Saturdays before noon are the best time to tour the island. Most Okinawan children on the island go to school on Saturday until noon. That differs from living in the United States. One time, we took part in a Walk-A-Thon of only about fourteen miles of the entire island. The walk was tiring, but enjoyable to see the scenery.

Walk-A-Thon

Commissary

We get our groceries at a place called a "Commissary.

Buying groceries for our family is an all-day affair.

Base Exchange

"The Base Exchange" is next to the Commissary. In

the hallways next to the Base Exchange, vendors sell all

kinds of unique items.

Other Kadena Facilities

There is a bank, barber shop, food court, dry-cleaners, eyeglass place, and other miscellaneous stores. Sometimes, we eat in the food court before going into the Base Exchange. On the base, there is also a Shoppette where we get gas and snacks.

Bank ATM Machine

Barber Shop

My dad and I get haircuts here. They cut them short, short, short for compliance with military haircut standards. I do not need it that short since I am not in the military.

Food Court

I Love To Eat Pizza and Doughnuts!

Base Theater

The military base has a theater. We must stand up for the National Anthem before the movie starts. They have good movies that are cheap, like $2.00 a movie. We always get popcorn and soda. If I am still hungry, I will get a candy bar just for good measure.

I Love Popcorn, Soda, and Candy!

Dry Cleaners

My dad gets his civilian coats, military coats, and military uniforms cleaned at the dry cleaners. His bosses want his uniform to be neat and pressed. He has camouflage uniforms, blue duty uniforms, and his dress blue coat for special occasions that the dry cleaners must clean and press. My favorite uniform he has is his camouflage clothing.

Vision Center and Optometrist

Every year, my family must get new glasses with our new prescription on them right after our optometry visit. My vision is not the best. The Optometrist diagnosed me as being near- sided and far- sided with a stigma- tism. I liked the glasses with blue frames I picked out at the Vision Center not the ones the worker showed me.

Arts and Crafts Center

I enjoy going to the Arts and Crafts Center, where I can work on art and pottery. My brother enjoys working on art projects. We only go once a week after school. I try different projects since I am not sure how creative I am. Right now, I am working on a bowl in pottery class.

Bowling Center

The local bowling center is where I am in a league. Bowling is enjoyable for me, and I am an expert at it. My brothers are also good at bowling, just like I am. I am in a bowling league because I get strikes. The name of our team is the "Pythons."

Youth Center

Sometimes, there are activities at the Youth Center where we can play foosball and other games. Teens at the center are enjoying the fun activities that the Youth Center offers. There are video games, television, foosball, board games, pool, and a library.

Base Pool

My favorite activity is to go swimming in the base pool when it is open. We can splash around in the pool and dive into the pool. It is five feet deep. We go to Open Swim Time on the weekend. I like to dive off at the end of the pool, but I do not do a belly flop.

Security Police

There are Security Police at the gates to check for authorization to enter the base. Security Police patrol, enforce the laws on base, and check buildings to make sure no one gets in the buildings that is not supposed to.

Flight Line

The flight line is amazing, with activity going on around the planes and maintenance workers trying to get the planes ready to leave the base. I get to see all kinds of planes leave the "runway" and flight line. Only planes authorized by the Control Tower Operator can be on the runway. If you try to go on the flight line without permission, the Security Policeman will arrest you.

It is so much fun watching planes fly off the runway. There are various planes on the runway. There are F-15 Eagles, MC-130J Commando II's, HH-60G Pave Hawk helicopters, MC-130H Combat Talon's, and the E-3 Sentry. At various times throughout the day, planes arrive at Kadena Air Base like the C-141 Starlifter, DC-9 Medivac, and C-17 Globemaster III. I like to watch mechanics working on the planes.

A Maintenance Worker On the Flight Line

This is an F-15 Eagle taking off the runway.

Pilots get to fly the plane. Sometimes, I will sit across the road from the flight line to watch the planes take off.

I enjoy watching the helicopters take off too. My dad got an incentive ride because of his exceptional job performance and got to fly in a helicopter over the Sea of Japan (East Sea). He said it scared him to hang his legs out the door of the helicopter until he felt con-

fident to do so. Dad said the Sea of Japan (East Sea) was

so beautiful.

Off Base Housing

Before we got to move on base, we lived in the bottom apartment on a big hill near the military base. The top floor was our property owner, "Fuji." The second floor was a manager for the Army and Air Force Exchange Service (A.A.F.E.S.). We lived on the bottom floor, which had metal bars on the window and a narrow driveway. We had to get a van since we had a large family. Dad had to have two types of car insurance both Japanese and American. The steering wheel was on the right side inside of the van. That took time adjusting to. It also took time to learn how to drive on the left side of the road. The roads here are different.

Our play area was small which was located next to the driveway. It was only like a couple of feet wide and had a brick wall next to it. If you fell over the wall, it was a long drop to the highway. Mom and dad stayed outdoors with us to make sure we kept away from the wall. Our house was so tiny as compared to an American house in the United States. Our couch in the living room bumped up against the dining room table. Geckos used to come into our house. They kept the mosquitoes out of the house and were friendly.

Because of the humidity, mildew happened in the house, so we had to put mothballs in our closet to protect our clothes and other valuables. The funniest thing happened when my mom went to play bingo on base. Dad had to babysit us. When he was cooking a roast, Dad put the wicker basket, the glass cookware, and the roast all into the oven. The wicker basket caught on fire. Mom was not happy. Dad was better at military service, but not at cooking.

We lived off base for a year before the Base Housing Office approved us to move on base. The family was extremely excited to be moving to the military base.

Our Base Housing

Our base housing is a two-story house with an upstairs and a downstairs. The house has metal doors, metal shutters, and thick windows. The stairs lead up to my room, which has a large window facing the street. Sometimes, we have a house cleaner come to our house once a week. Her name is Mrs. Kinjo. She is a genuinely nice Okinawan lady. The next-door neighbor is a Navy Seal who is gone almost 364 days during the year, so he hardly sees or gets to spend time with his family. My mom was also in the Navy too. We like playing with the kids' next door since they are about our age. Their daughter is fifteen, and their son is eleven.

Bad Weather

Most families would go to the Commissary when severe weather would occur to get flashlights, batteries, water, and food. Emergency supplies would run out at the Commissary. People bought all the emergency supplies at the store and the shelves were bare.

During a typhoon (which is like a hurricane just on water), all the metal doors, metal windows, and shutters were closed and locked by the family members tightly due to high winds. This was the most secure place for our family to be since there were no base shelters. Sometimes, we spent a week indoors without coming outside because of the typhoon. We went through nine typhoons while we were living on the island. The typhoon made the high winds pick up anything not placed inside the houses. Couches and motorcycles had flown around the base because of the fierce winds. They were dangerous and caused severe damage to the property.

There were no casualties or deaths.

Water Rationing

For one month, we had to conserve water because of a base- wide and island-wide "water rationing" scenario. We only flushed the toilet on certain days of the week. We had to fill up plastic containers with water and fill the bathtub with water. Also, we could not water our lawn or wash our car. My dad could get a ticket or an Article 15 Nonjudicial Punishment (this is punishment of a loss of a stripe and/or monetary fines) for watering the grass and not conserving water. We had a schedule during the week for the days we could use the water for baths, kitchen sink, and bathroom faucets.

Ouch! Ouch! Ouch!

We had to go to the base theater to get Japanese Encephalitis shots due to the number of mosquitoes on the island. Our family had to stand in line to wait for the medical staff to give us our shots. We ended up getting three shots each.

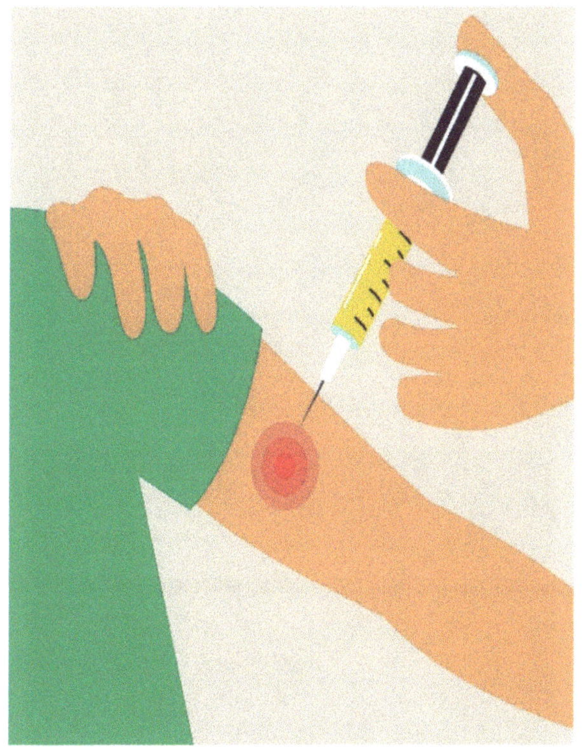

When I Grow Up!

When I grow up, I want to be a pilot, firefighter, police officer, or in the military. Who knows what the future will hold?

Pilot

Firefighter

Police Officer Making An Arrest

Proud of My Parents

I am proud that my mom and dad served their country in the military. My mom was an Air Force dependent, a Petty Officer 3rd Class in the Navy, and in the Navy Reserve. Dad was a Sergeant in the Air Force. They liked to serve in the military.

Adjusting to Being a Military Dependent

Sometimes, people do not realize that military dependents deal with emotional issues and separation anxiety. They must adjust under extreme circumstances like military duty, wartime, and other temporary duty assignments of their mom and/or dad.

This Is The Life of a Military Dependent!

Living on a military base, especially in a new country, is so much fun. We move around to different bases all over the world, so we get to see so many places and experience diverse cultures. It is hard though for me to adjust and keep friends. However, I love the experience of being a military dependent. Because we move, we keep assorted items still packed in boxes.

Effect of My Parents Military Service

My parents' military service affected what I became when I grew up. I wanted to serve my country in the military just as they did.

www.ingramcontent.com/pod-product-compliance
Lightning Source LLC
Chambersburg PA
CBHW040844010826
48978CB00012BB/895